Travels with My Family

Travels with my Family

BY *Marie-Louise Gay*
AND *David Homel*

(g)

GROUNDWOOD BOOKS / HOUSE OF ANANSI PRESS
TORONTO   BERKELEY

Groundwood Books / House of Anansi Press
groundwoodbooks.com

We gratefully acknowledge for their financial support of our publishing
program the Canada Council for the Arts, the Ontario Arts Council and
the Government of Canada.

 Canada Council Conseil des Arts
for the Arts du Canada

 ONTARIO ARTS COUNCIL
CONSEIL DES ARTS DE L'ONTARIO

With the participation of the Government of Canada
Avec la participation du gouvernement du Canada |

Library and Archives Canada Cataloguing in Publication
Gay, Marie-Louise
Travels with my family/ by Marie-Louise Gay and David Homel.
ISBN: 978-0-88899-688-6 (bound). – ISBN: 978-0-88899-833-0 (pbk.)
I. Homel, David II. Title.
PS8565.O6505T73 2006   jC813'.54   C2005-906566-4

Groundwood Books is committed to protecting our natural environment.
This book is printed on FSC®-certified paper, contains post-consumer fibers and other con-
trolled sources, is manufactured using renewable energy-biogas and processed chlorine-free.

Design by Michael Solomon
Printed in Canada

To our two boys

My Adventures

Heading out on the road...

W hen you hear the word "vacation," what do you think of? Beaches and warm water, nice hotels with swimming pools? Giant waterslides and amusement parks and miniature golf? Maybe even Disneyland? Me, too.

But not my parents. They're pretty strange that way. They want to have new adventures in some out-of-the-way place. So every vacation, my little brother and I have to go with them to some wild, faraway destination where no one else ever goes. The farther it is, the more remote it is, the better my parents like it.

That's called "off the beaten track." No tourist

traps, and no line-ups. No wonder! Nobody wants to go there!

Half the time, I end up having to save them, or my brother, or both, from alligators, high tides or sandstorms. Let me tell you, sometimes it's pretty tough.

I don't know why my parents are like that. I guess it's their way of feeling young again, and different from other people. If it were up to my little brother and me, we'd be normal kids with normal parents going on a normal vacation.

Even getting to where we're going can be an adventure. Like the time we drove to Maine.

"We'll take the road through the mountains," my father said, showing us the map. "It'll be much more interesting."

When he says "interesting," he really means we'll be driving on bumpy back roads, folding and unfolding the map, and generally getting lost.

"It'll be much more beautiful, too," my mother added. Which means we'll have to stop and look at all the beautiful stuff along the way. It'll take us forever.

So there we were, bumping along the winding mountain roads, on our way to Maine. Our tiny car was filled to the brim with suitcases, books and fishing nets. My parents' bicycles were on the roof and my brother's and mine were tied to the trunk.

Between us was our brand-new cat-carrying box with Miro, our cat, inside. It was about 100 degrees in the car. And 150 degrees in the box.

"Why is the cat's tongue hanging out?" my brother asked. "I thought only dogs did that."

"Maybe he thinks he's a dog," I said. Actually, he looked pretty sick. His furry face was pale, and his eyes were half-closed.

"It's too hot for him," my father said. "Let him out of the box. He'll be fine."

But he wasn't. First he gave a pitiful howl, then he threw up on the back seat. Then he climbed in front and peed on my mother's shoes.

The next thing we knew, a wasp flew in the

open window — our car doesn't have air-conditioning, of course — and stung my brother on the knee. He howled. Not a pitiful howl. A loud, angry howl that startled my father. He slammed on the brakes and the bikes fell off the trunk. The car in back of us started honking its horn and flashing its lights.

We pulled onto the side of the road. My father started attaching the bikes to the rack again while my mother put cream on my brother's knee.

Then Miro tried to escape. I couldn't blame him. He jumped out the car window and crawled under a blackberry bush. My brother was still crying. My father was still figuring out how to get the bikes back on the rack. And I wasn't allowed to get out of the car because it was too dangerous.

So it was up to my mother to capture him. She got down on her hands and knees, and in her soothing cat-voice, she started talking to Miro. People were laughing as they drove by. There was my mother, down on all fours, talking to a blackberry bush! But slowly, one step at a time, Miro crept out from under the bush, and my mother scooped him up in her arms. Then she ran for the car. I didn't want to tell her, but there were blackberry twigs in her hair.

It was going to be a long trip. A whole day of beautiful, winding mountain roads and scenic vistas. But we'd get to Maine, all right. Just in time for...

But you'll see. Another family vacation was about to begin.

ONE

In Maine, we are nearly flattened by Hurricane Bob

We had been hearing about Hurricane Bob on the radio all week long. After a while, I got pretty tired of it. How can you take a hurricane seriously when its name is Bob? No offense to people named Bob, but it's just not a very scary name.

If I was in charge of naming hurricanes, I would call them Hurricane Hulk, or Demon, or Destroyer. Now that would scare people!

We had rented a cottage right by the ocean. We were so close to the water that you could sit on the front porch and spit watermelon seeds into the Atlantic. Or almost.

And there were blueberry bushes, too, with tiny

fruit the size of a baby's fingernail. My brother and I picked the berries right off the bushes for breakfast.

The other fun things you could eat were the sea urchins that lived in the water. They were brown, prickly animals with poisonous spines. You smashed them open with a hatchet, and there was an orange part inside that supposedly tasted really good, like the ocean. Or so my father said. I tried one, and that was enough. My brother pretended to throw up just looking at them.

Our cat, Miro, loved Maine. It was a lot better than being in a boiling hot car. He had never been to the sea before. Every evening, he went down to the pebbly beach to chase the little green crabs that lived there. When he caught one, or, should I say, when one caught him by pinching his nose, he wished he hadn't, because crabs never let go. But Miro never learned. He caught furry brown wood mice, too, and left them on the porch in front of the door. My mother would scream every time she stepped on one in her bare feet, first thing in the morning.

Miro always looked miffed when she did that. After all, he was giving her a present. It's funny, because my mother usually loves surprises and presents. When my brother gives her a bunch of dandelions, for example, even if they're half crushed, she always looks so pleased. I guess dead mice aren't at the top of her list of favorite things.

The radio told us that Hurricane Bob was moving up the eastern shore of the United States. First he was going to hit Florida. Then Bob changed his mind and decided to go for North Carolina. No, not there. Why not try a little farther up the coast? Like Maine. No hurricanes ever went there. He'd have the place to himself.

"Hurricanes like it hot," my father told us. He was always explaining useful bits of knowledge to us. "They're tropical storms. The water here is too cold for them. Nobody even swims in this water."

It was true. The water in Maine was so cold you couldn't put both feet in at the same time. A

minute in this water and your skin would turn blue. My brother was the only one who didn't feel the cold. Maybe he'd been a polar bear in another life.

"But the radio says the hurricane's coming here," my mother said.

"The radio is just trying to scare us," my father told her. He was always telling us that we shouldn't believe everything we heard on the TV and the radio.

"But if it'll make you feel safer, we'll go into town for some supplies."

"I'd feel safer if you paid attention to the radio once in a while," she answered, smiling. "Now let's go!"

There was an enormous crowd in front of the Blue Hill General Store and Hardware. The parking lot was full of pick-up trucks with lobster traps in the back. Men in lumberjack shirts were leaving the store, carrying big sheets of plywood. Their wives were carrying huge cardboard boxes. Everybody was looking anxiously up at the sky.

"Are those men going to build a house?" my brother asked.

"Not exactly," I told him. "The wood is for covering the windows and doors when the hurricane comes."

"Oh," he said. Then he peered anxiously at the sky, too.

A moment later, he asked, "What do you think those ladies have in their boxes?"

"The usual things," I said, as if I prepared for hurricanes every day. "Batteries, flashlights, candles. Duct tape."

"Duck tape?"

"Sure," I told him. "If you have a duck, and he asks too many questions about Hurricane Bob, you can tape his beak shut."

"Stop teasing your brother!" my mother ordered.

She was pretty nervous. It must have been Hurricane Bob's fault.

In the end, we came home with practically nothing. I was disappointed. Everyone else was driving away with big sheets of plywood and boxes of heavy-duty batteries. And us? Just some scented dinner candles, a couple of gallon jugs of water and two little packs of batteries for the radio and the flashlight.

Were we getting ready for a hurricane or not?

My mother sat next to the radio, reading a book. I don't know how anyone can concentrate when the radio is screaming away full blast about hurricanes, and thousand-mile-an-hour winds.

She wasn't really reading anyway. She was just pretending. After she got tired of pretending, she went out on the front porch with a determined look on her face. My father was there, watching the waves crash on the rocks. You couldn't spit a watermelon seed into the ocean anymore. The wind would blow it back in your face.

My mother must have convinced my father that we should at least prepare a little for the hurricane, because when they came back in, things started happening. My father filled the bathtub with water. My mother filled up all the pots and pans, and put covers on them. Then he went outside and turned the car around so it was facing the road, in case we had to leave in a hurry.

"Put all your favorite things near the door," my father said. "You never know, we might decide to leave."

I didn't think we would be doing the deciding. Bob would. I piled my Discman, my baseball cards and my binoculars by the door. My brother put his stuffed penguin on top.

"Look, the neighbors are going!" he shouted. "Do you think we should, too?"

Along the shore, just a stone's throw away, was another cottage, just as close to the water as ours. The people living there had packed all their things in their car, and they were driving away.

"Are you scared?" I asked my brother.

"Me? No way! It's only a hurricane."

But he didn't sound very sure. His voice was a little squeaky. And he went over to the door to check on his penguin.

All of a sudden it started to rain. It had been raining before, off and on, a normal sort of rain. But now the wind started blowing and the rain came in sideways and made a terrible racket on the roof.

"Great!" my father said, rubbing his hands together. "We'll see if this guy Bob's the real thing or not."

"What if he is?" I asked.

"Come and look!" my brother shouted.

The waves had swallowed up the shore. The pebbly beach where Miro hunted crabs had completely disappeared.

And that's when the electricity went off.

"I was expecting that," my father told us.

"We were all expecting it," my mother groaned. "There's a hurricane out there, in case you haven't noticed."

My father opened the pack of batteries and put two in the radio.

"We won't listen to the radio all the time," he explained, "in order to save the batteries. Anyway, the radio is driving us all crazy."

"Hurricane Bob! Hurricane Bob!" my little brother started shouting. When he pinched his nose with his fingers, he sounded just like the announcer on the radio.

"Stop that racket!" my father told us.

My brother and I looked at each other. We started laughing. The wind was roaring. The waves were crashing on the rocks right in front of the house. The rain was hammering on the windows. The radio was screaming at us. We could hardly hear ourselves think. Here we were, in the middle of a hurricane, and our father tells us to be quiet!

We decided to go out on the porch and watch the waves. The water was gray and angry-looking. The pine trees were rocking in the wind. Miro was in the window behind us, looking worried. When a big wave hit the rocks right in front of the house, he jumped into the air, then dove under the sofa. That was another useful scientific fact my father had taught us. Animals can feel the low pressure brought by big storms, and they don't like it at all.

My brother stared up at the howling trees. "I think they're going to take off."

Then he put his arms out like wings, and let the wind grab him.

"I can fly!" he shouted.

A great gust of wind picked him up. He was flying! The next thing he knew, he was in the meadow in front of the house, lying on his stomach, with his nose in the tall grass.

He tried to get up, but the wind pushed him down again. I pulled him to his feet. It was raining so hard we could scarcely see the house, a few feet away.

"We're getting soaked," I said. "Let's go inside."

"I don't want to. I like flying." But I dragged him inside anyway.

My parents had started a fire in the fireplace. Every so often, the wind blew the smoke back down the chimney and into the living room, and we all started coughing. But that was where we spent the rest of the afternoon, and the night, too. The wind blew, the walls creaked, and there were times I thought the roof would fly away. Miro was hiding somewhere, probably still under the couch. I put some food in his bowl, but he didn't come out. He must have really been scared, since he can't resist a snack.

We heard that Bob was supposed to hit us — the announcer called that "landfall" — in the middle of the night. Every once in a while, my mother would get up, go to the front window, turn on the flashlight and point it into the darkness. But it was useless. Everything was pitch black.

It was the longest night of my life. But not for my brother. He fell asleep. He didn't even hear the enormous *crack!* in the middle of the night.

"What was that?" my mother yelled.

We rushed to the window, my mother, my father and I.

"I can't see a thing," said my father.

"Is the world still out there?" my mother wondered.

Sometimes I think she reads too much science fiction. Of course the world was still out there — wasn't it?

The next morning, the sun was shining weakly. My brother woke me up. I had fallen asleep in the chair. I opened my eyes and saw Miro on my lap.

"Hey, what happened? Didn't Hurricane Bob get us?"

Miro jumped off my lap. He walked over to his bowl and started eating breakfast. I could hear him purring. Everything was normal again.

We went outside. The ocean had gone back to where it was supposed to be.

Then we went around to the side of the house.

"There's something wrong with our tree," my brother said.

He was right. The pine tree closest to the house looked as though it had been turned inside out by the wind, like a giant umbrella.

Then I saw what had made the noise during the night.

Hurricane Bob had knocked over the enormous pine tree in front of our neighbors' cottage. Its roots were hanging in the air. The tree had crashed through the porch and flattened the front of their house. It looked like a bunch of pick-up sticks.

"What if that had been us?" my brother wondered.

"Well, it wasn't," I said. "We made it! We survived the hurricane."

"And without duck tape!"

I started making quacking noises in his ear. He pinched his nose with his fingers and shouted, "Hurricane Bob! Hurricane Bob!" Then he chased me across the wet field.

I guess a hurricane isn't so bad, as long as the trees don't fall on you. It helps to have good luck if you want to have adventures — that's what I learned that night.

TWO
My brother nearly drowns off Tybee Island

I liked Maine, Hurricane Bob and all, but there was only one problem. The water was so cold there were practically icebergs floating in it. We decided to drive south, where the water is as warm as a bathtub, and where we could go swimming every day.

"I don't think Miro could take the trip," my father said. "Going to Maine was bad enough."

"He can stay at your grandmother's," my mother told my brother and me. "You'll see, he'll love it there. He can chase the squirrels around the backyard."

So Miro would have his own vacation, without

us. We drove him back to my grandmother's house. We promised to send him lots of postcards, and my brother nearly hugged him to death. But when we left, Miro was already sniffing around my grandmother's kitchen, with a smile on his face.

I wondered what my parents were going to dream up for this trip. You have to admit, a front-row seat at a hurricane is pretty hard to beat. But when we left the land behind and started driving across the water, I knew we were in for something special.

The road went on for miles and miles with nothing but the sea on all sides, and just a few lonely telephone poles stringing electrical wires over the water.

"This has got to be the longest bridge in the world!" my little brother said.

"It's called a causeway," my father told us.

My brother crossed his arms and sat back on the seat. "It looks like a bridge to me."

"It looks like a silver ribbon floating on the ocean," my mother sighed happily. "It's beautiful."

"It's a bridge," said my brother, sticking his lower lip out.

That's the way we are in my family sometimes. Everybody has to be right.

The sky was bright blue, and the water was as calm as Miro when he's asleep. Then I remembered

Hurricane Bob. If ever a few strong waves rose up, the road would disappear in no time.

But that was the chance we had to take to get to the house we had rented on Tybee Island, in the state of Georgia. A wooden house that stood on stilts with a few palm trees around it, and miles and miles of beaches.

It turned out to be a great summer for needlefish ice cream cones. They're real easy to make. You need a sandy beach, and a lot of those tiny fish with sharp, pointy noses like miniature swordfish. You grab a fish by its tail, stick its nose into a mud-ball and — presto! — you have a needlefish ice-cream cone.

Then, of course, you walk around and pretend to lick it. You should see the looks you get from grownups!

And it doesn't hurt the fish because they're already dead, caught in the fishermen's nets along with the mudballs.

We also made jellyfish porcupines. You need one dead jellyfish lying on the beach, and a hand-ful of sticks.

We had lots of work that summer, my little brother and I, taking the needlefish out of the fishermen's nets.

"You got them itty-bitty fingers," the fishermen

told us. "You kids can slip them fingers of yours right in between the loops of them nets and pull them critters right out."

My brother stared at the fishermen with their big blunt fingers and their sunburnt faces and their tattoos. He didn't know what to think. But I did. I knew that a critter was an animal, and that we had just gotten ourselves a vacation job. We got paid a nickel a needlefish, and pretty soon my brother and I had enough to buy real ice cream cones. Pecan was my favorite flavor.

One day my father went fishing for crabs with some men he had met on the beach. I wanted to go, too, but he said there was no room in the boat for me. But how much room do I take up? I guess he wanted to have his own adventure without me. So I was left behind with my brother and my mother.

I was pretty mad, and pretty bored. I went down to the beach by myself. I wished Miro was there. He could have kept me entertained by chasing the little transparent crabs that disappeared into holes in the sand when I got too close to them. I read all the notices on the notice board at the edge of the beach. There were ads for nature walks at sunset with a guide. Who needed a guide just to walk along the beach? Then there was a notice for a lost dog. "Lost: one fat beagle," it said. "Name: Ninny. Place: Oceanville Cemetery." I couldn't believe that anyone would name his dog Ninny, and admit in public that it was fat. And anyway, how does a dog get lost in a cemetery? Unless it got kidnapped by a ghost?

I saw dolphins jumping out of the water, so close to the shore that you could hear the noises they made. People say that dolphins sing beautiful songs, but they sounded more like old men blowing their noses to me. But maybe they sounded that way because I was mad about not being able to go fishing.

Then I saw Mr. Sandcastle at his usual spot. Not too many grownups build sandcastles unless they have kids, but Mr. Sandcastle was different.

He was a very big man with small, delicate hands, and he was famous for his castles. They were huge, with turrets, drawbridges and moats. You could almost picture the tiny sand-colored knights riding out of the castle, off on a quest. Mr. Sandcastle even spray-painted the walls and turrets with colors from aerosol cans, and he didn't seem to care that the waves swept the castles away after he'd finished building them.

I was poking at a washed-up jellyfish with a piece of driftwood when suddenly I heard my mother screaming all the way from the porch of our house. She was standing on a chair and slapping at her hair and arms and legs. That was nothing special. She screamed every time a palmetto bug fell off the roof and landed on her.

I think palmetto bugs are cool. They look like gigantic cockroaches wearing black, shiny helmets. My brother and I were always trying to catch one. We built traps with driftwood and seaweed. We wanted to train them to do tricks, like jumping through hoops or tightrope-walking. But the bugs were much too fast.

After she calmed down, my mother told my brother and me that we were going to go on a sand-dollar hunt. My brother was excited. Maybe he thought that sand dollars were real money. But I knew better.

Pretty soon we were wading through the warm water over to Little Tybee Island. It's the kind of island that disappears when the tide is high. But when the tide is low, it comes back out of the water, like magic. Actually, Little Tybee Island is the bottom of the sea when the tide goes out.

If my father had been there, he would have explained all about how the tides worked. But not my mother. She wandered around the island, daydreaming and looking at the pelicans flying low over the water, collecting shells and bits of driftwood, and probably getting ideas for the drawings she does. Meanwhile, I was working hard as usual, gathering up sand dollars and putting them in a plastic bag with holes in it for the water to run out, My brother splashed in the warm tidal pools like a baby seal.

A little while later, I looked up. All around us, Little Tybee Island was starting to shrink. The water was gobbling up the sand. We were the only ones out there now. Meanwhile, my mother was still daydreaming.

But I saw what was happening. Our little island of sand was being cut off from the beach by a deep channel of rushing water, and it was growing deeper by the minute. Soon the whole Atlantic Ocean would separate us from our house. And my little brother didn't know how to swim.

"Hey, Mom," I called, and I pointed to the water all around us.

Her dreamy face changed in a hurry. She dropped all her shells.

"Everybody stay calm!" she screamed. "We have to head back — right now!"

We had to get back across the channel. Quickly, my mother decided that she would hold my brother under one arm and swim with the other. I was supposed to hang on to her back and kick my legs as hard as I could.

First, I stuffed my bag of sand dollars into my bathing suit. Then I grabbed her shoulder. The next thing I knew, we were fighting our way through the rushing current of the channel. Soon, the water was way over our heads.

For every stroke we took to move forward, the current pushed us two strokes to the side. At that rate, I figured we'd end up in South America. Silver mullets flew past us, chased by the dolphins. My brother's eyes were wide as saucers and luckily, for once, he kept his mouth shut. I pumped my legs up and down, and held on tight to my mother. The ferocious current crashed around our ears. But inch by inch, we moved closer to the shore.

Finally, we made it. All three of us flopped on the beach, panting like exhausted starfish. I shook

the water out of my eyes and looked up. There was
my father. On the sand next to him was a big bas-
ket of blue, crawly crabs.

"You look like something the cat dragged in!"
he said.

My father's really clueless sometimes.

"While you three were relaxing on the beach, I
was working hard for our supper," he added with
a proud smile.

My mother and I just rolled our eyes.

"Not crabs again," my brother said. "I want hot
dogs!"

I wanted to show my father my sand dollar collection. I fished in my bathing suit, but the current had swept them away, bag and all.

Oh, well. At least I'd saved my mother and my brother. And I'd had a real adventure of my own, too.

THREE

Alligators nearly devour us in the swamps of Florida

After we had to swim for our lives that day, we were more careful with the ocean. My mother cut a page out of the newspaper that gave the times for the tides, high tide and low, for the rest of the month. The water wasn't going to sneak up on us again.

After a while, my father started saying that he had itchy feet. Which means he was thinking about going somewhere new. So instead of scratching his feet, he did what he always does at a time like that. He took out his road map.

"Look, Florida's not far at all. It's almost next door. And I've never been there."

Florida? My brother and I looked at each other. We couldn't believe our ears!

"*Disneyland!*" we shouted.

You see, we were normal, my brother and I, even if our parents weren't.

But Disneyland was too normal for my parents. Too much like everybody else, too ordinary. Not original enough. Somehow I wasn't surprised.

"Why would you want to have a fake adventure in a theme park with plastic alligators?" my father wanted to know. "I'll show you real alligators. And they won't be made out of plastic, no, sir!"

So it was off to Okefenokee Swamp, to go canoeing. The little bit of the swamp that hangs down into the state of Florida.

I don't think anyone else has ever even heard of Okefenokee Swamp. I don't think anyone can even say it. Except for my mother, who told us about a comic strip called Pogo that had possums and alligators and skunks that could talk. They all lived in the Okefenokee Swamp.

"*We have met the enemy, and he is us!* That's what Pogo used to say," my mother told us.

My brother and I laughed, even if we weren't quite sure what Pogo meant. Or my mother, either.

There we were in our boiling-hot car, with the windows rolled down, heading to Florida. I thought of Miro. He was probably relaxing under a tree in my grandmother's cool backyard. He was lucky.

Not like us. We were the only ones on the road. Everyone else was sleeping off the heat on their front-porch swings, or in hammocks under the trees, waiting for the sun to go down and things to cool off.

Meanwhile, we were in a big hurry to get to a swamp.

The problem with traveling in a car is that there's nothing to do. At first my mother played Twenty Questions with us. But my brother got mad because I guessed his animal too quickly. It was a penguin. It was too easy. There he was, sitting with his stuffed penguin on his lap. Category: animal. Color: black and white. Anyone could have guessed that, since penguins are his all-time favorite animal.

To calm him down, my mother said we would play the Alphabet Game. We had to look out the window and spot things that started with the different letters of the alphabet. A was for airplane, B was for billboard, C was for cow, D was for… We got stuck at D. When my brother pointed at me and said, "I see a dummy!" it was my turn to get mad. "E!" I shouted. "I see an egghead." I elbowed him. He elbowed me back.

"F!" yelled my father. "F is for finished. The game is finished!"

That put an end to the game.

"I'm hungry," my brother complained after we'd stopped yelling at each other.

"We're almost there," my father told him. "Can't you wait?"

"I'm hungry, too," I said.

"The next time we stop for gas," my father promised.

He found a baseball game on the radio. The Atlanta Braves were playing the Chicago Cubs, and nothing else mattered. When my father wants to get somewhere, he won't stop for anything, unless it's a full-blown emergency. We could starve to death and he wouldn't notice. On we drove.

The next day, bright and early, there we were, all four of us in a canoe with our lunch in a cooler, and a park ranger looking at us as if we were about to become some alligator's dessert.

"Whatever you do, don't put your hands in the water," he said.

He wore a Smokey the Bear hat and mirrored

sunglasses, like a bad guy in the movies. Except he was supposed to be a good guy.

"And if you don't like your sandwich, kids, eat it anyway, because if you throw it over the edge, it'll attract them gators something fierce. And you don't want that!"

My mother was looking pretty nervous. When she gets nervous, she goes completely quiet. She even forgets to point out all the beautiful things around us. My father, who wanted us to have an authentic adventure with real live alligators, was smiling happily. He slung his binoculars around his neck and checked the film in his camera. I wondered whether my little brother was going to throw his sandwich overboard anyway, just to see if what the ranger said was true, and if I was going to have to save him again.

The thing you need to know about Okefenokee Swamp is that everything is always moving. The islands aren't nailed down. They turn around and around in circles, floating in the water. That's what Okefenokee means: the trembling land. I read that in the little pamphlet we got from the park ranger. I was reading to keep from thinking about what was going to happen on our authentic adventure. To keep from trembling, like the islands turning circles around us.

Which would be worse: getting lost forever

among the floating islands, or getting eaten by alligators? And would we even have a choice?

We started paddling into the swamp. We were the only canoe on the water. That couldn't be a good sign.

Suddenly my mother, who was paddling in the front of the canoe, started waving her hands in the air and pointing. Something was in the water, dead ahead of us.

"An alligator!" she whispered, as if she were afraid it would hear. I don't even know if alligators have ears.

"Nonsense," my father told her. "That's just a log."

He couldn't see it from where he was, at the back of the canoe. "You're the navigator, we're counting on you to guide us," he'd told my mother when we left the dock. But I guess she wasn't the navigator when it came to spotting alligators.

We kept on paddling, right over the top of the alligator. A second later, it popped up again, behind us, bobbing in the water. Sure enough, it was a log. Score one for my father.

Once the alligator turned out to be a log, I relaxed a little bit. Big water lilies floated by, with yellow and pink and white flowers. There were rows of painted turtles on the logs, all lined up, from big to little. When we came near, they

splashed into the water in the same order, from biggest to littlest. My mother must have relaxed, too. She started saying how beautiful everything was. Standing in the swamp, white egrets stared at us with their strange yellow eyes. My father was taking pictures of everything.

I watched the islands floating past. Looking at them, you couldn't tell they were moving. In the Okefenokee Swamp, there were at least twenty-five different plants that you could eat if you got lost — I read that in the pamphlet the park ranger gave me. I wondered how lily pad sandwiches would taste.

Suddenly, my mother turned to me again and pointed at something.

"I suppose that's a log, too?" she whispered.

Right in front of us, lolling in the water, was something long and brown, with ridges on its back, its snout just out of the water, and two cold beady eyes.

"Dad," I said as calmly as I could. And I pointed straight ahead, too.

"That's just another log," he said. "Keep paddling, nice and easy."

"If it's just a log, then why does it have two..."

That's when our authentic alligator adventure began.

Just before we reached it, the "log," if you

believe my father, sank down into the water. But not all the way down. We paddled right over the top of it.

Scritchhhh — right over the razor-sharp scales on its back. My brother heard the sound, and he stared down at the floor of the canoe, his eyes bulging and his face very pale. We rose out of the water, ever so slightly — I swear we did.

My little brother started to stand up, as if he wanted to start running. Never stand in a canoe. Everybody knows that. Just in time, I grabbed him and sat him down again, and we both looked behind the canoe.

The alligator bobbed up again in the water, right where he had been. He had this look in his eye, as if he was just a little bit irritated. And a little bit hungry, too.

"See," my father said cheerfully, and a little too

loudly, "I told you we'd have a real-life alligator adventure, with real alligators. No Disneyland for us, no, sir!"

Then he started paddling fast — very fast — away from the alligator. We headed for a big island, and solid ground.

And what was basking in the sun on the shore of that island? You guessed it. An alligator as big as our car.

My mother gasped.

We made a quick U-turn. And started paddling like the wind.

I wasn't too surprised when, a few minutes later, a few scary silent minutes, my father looked at his watch and decided it was time to head back to the dock.

"Let's go for barbecue," he said brightly. "I'm still hungry. These sandwiches aren't enough for me."

But I knew better. And so did my little brother.

My mother just smiled and started whistling a tune.

By the way, I had a fried alligator tail sandwich for lunch. It was pretty good! And my dad was right. They weren't plastic alligators at all.

FOUR

We are nearly trampled and eaten by a herd of farm animals on Salt Spring Island

*I*f you ever want to do something really boring, try sitting in a room watching grownups listening to other grownups reading stories from a book. I know, I've tried it.

You see, my brother and I had to go all the way to British Columbia, on the Pacific Ocean, on the other side of the continent, to listen to my parents read their stories to crowds of people. That's part of their job, or so they say. If you ask me, I'd rather read a book by myself.

The place was so far we had to take an airplane.

"I'm afraid we can't bring Miro," my father

explained. "He wouldn't like it, being locked up in a cage in the baggage compartment."

"Besides," my mother added, "afterwards we're going to a farm to see some friends. You'll like them very much, I'm sure. But I'm afraid Miro might not get along with the other animals."

Maybe it was better that way. I'm sure Miro would have been bored silly listening to grownups reading stories to each other. Just the way my brother and I were. There was one cool part, though. We got to take a float plane.

A float plane can take off and land on water. Instead of wheels, it lands on something called pontoons. The plane was so small that our family filled it up completely. Just us and the pilot.

My brother and I drew straws to see who would sit in front with the pilot. I won!

The plane flew low over the water. We were so close we could almost see the fish in the ocean. The engine made so much noise we had to wear big earmuffs to protect our ears.

"Hey, isn't that a whale down there?" I shouted.

I pointed down to the water. But my brother ignored me. He was still mad that he had to sit in back with my parents.

We circled over an island and landed on the water. Then we floated over to the dock. We stepped out of the plane and pulled off our ear-muffs. There we were, on Salt Spring Island.

"It will be great to be on a farm," my mother said happily. "We'll have some peace and quiet in the country. It's really beautiful there."

My brother and I couldn't believe it. Were we really going to have a quiet, ordinary vacation for once?

"A farm? Like Old McDonald's? With horses and cows and stuff?" my brother asked.

"This farm is a little different," my father said.

Uh-oh! My little brother and I looked at each other and rolled our eyes. But we didn't say any-thing. If it wasn't going to be a normal farm with cows and chickens and a farmer in overalls with a pitchfork, what was it going to be?

We found out soon enough.

Our very first morning on the farm, we were woken up by gunshot blasts. *Bang! Bang! Bang!* just outside our bedroom window.

My brother and I jumped out of bed and ran to look. *Bang!* We crouched down and peered over the windowsill. There was George, our par-ents' friend, shooting at the sky with a big shot-gun.

"Blasted ravens!" he said. "I won't have you hurting my lambs, you varmints."

He fired another couple of shots at a big pine tree. *Bang! Bang!* Then he looked up at us and winked.

"Those blasted ravens try and peck my poor lambs' eyes out. They're absolute pests. You've gotta scare them off!"

Then he shouldered his shotgun and walked away, chuckling to himself.

My brother and I looked at each other. This was definitely not Old McDonald's Farm. It was going to be different.

Later, we were having breakfast when something bit my elbow. Ouch! I dropped my spoon. Whatever it was bit my other elbow, twice as hard.

I looked around. There were peacocks in the kitchen. I know what you're thinking. How magnificent, all those feathers, all those colors, peacocks are so beautiful — you sound just like my mother. But let me tell you, peacocks are about as friendly as rattlesnakes.

I jumped up, and some of my cereal ended up on the floor.

"You don't have to feed the peacocks, kids. All that granola's not good for them anyway! Ajax, Olive, get out of there!" George laughed.

I never knew that farmers kept their livestock in the kitchen.

There was an uproar under the table as the peacocks fought over the granola. My little brother sat stiffly on his chair, with both legs folded tightly underneath him, trying to stay out of the battle. Now if only Miro were there. He would have protected us from the birds. At least I think so.

Just then, the phone rang.

"George, it's for you!" yelled a shrill voice.

George went to answer the phone.

"Hello? Hello?" he shouted into the phone. Then he slammed it down.

A minute later he returned with a large gray parrot perched on his shoulder. He looked more like a pirate than a farmer.

"Confounded bird!" he mumbled to himself. The peacocks looked offended and walked out of the room. Maybe they thought he was talking about them.

But George was talking about Tuco — that was the parrot's name. Tuco could imitate ringing telephones and voices. He loved playing tricks, and George fell for them every time.

"Confounded bird!" squawked Tuco.

"Does he repeat everything?" my brother asked.

"Does he repeat everything?" squawked Tuco.

My brother gave the parrot a nasty look, because nobody likes being imitated. We soon learned that Tuco knew a lot of words. But I can't repeat them here.

In the country, there's supposed to be peace and quiet. Well, the peace and quiet lasted another minute or two, until George looked out the front window.

"Jackson!" he shouted.

Then he ran out the door with Tuco clinging to his shoulder, squawking, "Jackson! Jackson! Jackson!"

"Who's Jackson?" my little brother asked.

"I don't know." I took a quick look under the table. The coast was clear. "So far, we've seen a raven, a parrot and some peacocks. Maybe Jackson is a penguin. Let's go see."

My brother jumped up and ran outside, a big smile on his face. Penguins, as you know, are his favorite birds.

We made it outside without being attacked by the peacocks. We passed the garden, then went along the driveway. I saw something large and black galloping down the middle of the dirt road that ran in front of the farm.

So that was Jackson — he was a horse. And George was running after him, waving his arms.

Jackson the horse liked to play games, just like Tuco did. He pretended to be very interested in eating the grass by the side of the road. But every time George got close, and tried to grab him to take him back to the meadow on the other side of the fence, he galloped three or four steps farther on, and went back to eating some more grass.

Little by little, we were exploring the whole island, in slow motion, with Jackson leading the way, and George, Tuco, my brother and I following in single file.

"He was a circus horse," George told us. "When he retired, we took him in."

"What did he do in the circus?" asked my brother.

"He was a clown," George answered. "He still thinks he's pretty funny."

I wondered how George knew what his horse was thinking. Maybe you learned that in farm school.

"Maybe he thinks he's still in the circus," my brother suggested.

"This is a circus," George declared. "The whole farm is a circus, starring Jackson the Horse."

"And Tuco!" the parrot added loudly.

After a while, Jackson decided it was time to be caught. He probably wanted to eat something else, like oats, or apples. Grass must get pretty boring after a while. George took his bridle and we all walked down the dirt road, back to the farm.

There, we saw another strange sight.

"What on earth is your mother doing?"

We all stopped and stared. My mother was standing in the middle of the pen, surrounded by sheep. She was holding her drawing pad up in the air.

"She's drawing sheep, I guess."

My mother draws all the time. She'll draw anything, even smelly, wooly sheep.

My mother pushed the sheep away, walked to the other end of the meadow and started drawing. The sheep followed her, baa-ing loudly. They were playing the opposite game from Jackson the horse. Every time my mother moved away to get the right perspective to draw them, the sheep crowded closer to her. Maybe they wanted to learn how to be artists.

They were watching her from very close up, as

if they needed glasses. One of them put his nose right on her drawing pad, as if he wanted to help out.

"That's Velcro for you! He wants to be part of everything," George snorted. "We call him that because he sticks to you like a burr on a dog. Come on, boys, let's save your mother from being trampled to death!"

George opened the gate, and we went into the sheep pen with Jackson.

"Give the lady some room, you incorrigible lot of fleabags!" George told them. And he gave them a few taps on their wooly rear ends.

"Thanks, George," my mother said. I looked at her pad. She hadn't gotten very far, and there was sheep drool on the paper. "You should really brush their teeth once in a while. Whew!"

George laughed and patted Velcro. "I'll keep that in mind. I'm sure Velcro would love having his teeth brushed."

My mother sat down to draw again. We were enjoying the peace and quiet when, thirty seconds later, I heard my little brother cry for help.

How did he do it? I'll never know. But he managed to get his head stuck in the fence. And you know by now how curious sheep are, and how

when one sheep does something, they all want to do it. Velcro came over to see what the problem was, followed by Einstein, Cleopatra, Sneaker and Rocky 4, and pretty soon my brother had a couple dozen sheep around him, all trying to figure out what this new animal was doing in their meadow, and did he want to eat their grass, and was it really greener on the other side of the fence?

Velcro started to lick my brother's left ear.

"*Help!*"

"Don't panic there, lad. You're getting your ears cleaned for free."

George was as strong as a farmer is supposed to be. Still, I helped him lift the top log of the wood fence, and my little brother squirmed free.

"I hate sheep!"

"They were just being friendly," my mother said.

But I wasn't so sure. My friends don't lick my ears.

Just then my father showed up. He had been upstairs in the house, in George's office, checking his e-mail messages. He looked at us standing around my brother, who still had tears in his eyes. Jackson the horse was munching on George's straw hat. The sheep had surrounded us again, and were baa-ing as loudly as ever. The peacocks screeched from their perch on the fence.

Just then, Tuco started imitating a phone ringing.

"Did I miss anything?" my father asked.

"Not really," I said. "But maybe you should go answer the phone."

"Okay," he agreed, and ran back into the house.

I think even the sheep were laughing.

FIVE

Our parents nearly abandon us on a beach in California, where my brother is nearly swept out to sea by a sneaker wave

There's one good thing about having strange parents like mine. You get to travel a lot. You never have any trouble writing the "What I Did on My Summer Vacation" essay that you have to write every September in school. Sometimes the teachers tell me I must be making this stuff up, and I can't really blame them.

My mother was still laughing at my father over the trick Tuco played on him when we reached California, a few days after we left George's farm. The first thing you need to know about California is that the whole state is about to fall into the ocean. It really is true. We went to a place north of San Francisco to see a big crack in the ground, where a shaker — that's what they call earthquakes out there — split the earth in two about a hundred years ago. We also saw a set of railroad tracks that swerve like a snake, as if a giant had picked them up with his bare hands and twisted them. Those are the kinds of things an earthquake can do.

"What'll we do if California falls into the ocean when we're on it?" my brother asked.

"It won't happen," I told him.

We all peered into the giant crack in the ground. You couldn't even see the bottom. My mother held my brother's hand very tightly. As if anyone would want to jump in!

"I wonder what fell into that crack?" my brother asked, trying to lean over.

"Horses," said my father. "Trees, houses, people, anything that was near."

"It's really dark in there," my brother said, worried. "I wouldn't want to get swallowed up."

My brother worries a lot. I think he takes after my mother.

But he was right. It was pretty dark in that crack.

"Animals know there's going to be an earthquake before humans do," I told him. "So if you see some animals acting strange, you know you have to be careful."

My brother looked very hard at a cow that was grazing in the next field. "Is that cow acting strange?" he asked.

"It's acting perfectly normal," I said. "For a cow."

After we visited the crack in the ground and the swervy railroad tracks, our parents decided we should go to the seaside. The second thing you need to know about California is that it's not always warm and sunny. You've seen those television shows, right, with all the palm trees and the sunshine? Well, there's not a single palm tree around Punta Reyes, near the big crack in the ground. That's because there's too much fog, and you need lots of sunshine for palm trees.

I suppose that if you asked my parents, they'd say that fog is much more interesting than sunshine. "More mysterious," my father would say. "More romantic," my mother would add.

It was chilly and foggy, and we had to put sweaters on. But I have to admit, there were plenty of cool things to see. Every time the tide goes out, it leaves behind all kinds of starfish and mussels and sea cucumbers in the pools in between the rocks.

"We're going exploring, too," my father said. "Have fun, we'll be back soon!"

Then he and my mother walked away.

But we were too busy watching a starfish drill a hole in a mussel shell to pay much attention.

"Hey, look!" my brother shouted. "That starfish has only four arms."

"Don't worry, it'll grow a new one back."

"Starfish can grow arms? How do they do that?"

"I don't know," I admitted. "It must be all the vitamins in the seaweed."

My brother started squeezing the little bubbles of air that seaweed uses to stay on top of the water. No matter how hard he squeezed, the bubbles wouldn't burst. They were as tough as old leather boots.

The rocks were covered with greenish-black plants. And when those plants got wet, they were as slippery as ice. And sure enough, my brother slipped and landed on his seat in the slimy sea-weed. I helped him up.

"Hey, where are Mom and Dad?" he asked.

We both looked around. The beach was desert-ed for as far as we could see. Long curls of fog were rolling in from the sea and reaching onto the land. They looked like witches' fingers that had come to grab us. We jumped off the rocks and ran back towards the beach. No one was there, either. Just great piles of rocks and the waves coming in underneath the fog.

"I don't see them," I told my brother.

"I think they ran away."

"Why would they do that?"

"I think they abandoned us," he said. "You know, like in Hansel and Gretel."

Then my brother panicked. He started running down the beach, between the giant rocks, jumping over the tide pools. He didn't really know where he was going. He was too scared to think. I was scared, too, but not so scared that I didn't keep my eyes open.

That's why I saw it before my brother did. The wave.

A wave that was much bigger than all the others came out of nowhere and crashed right into him, like a football player tackling someone. My brother fell onto the rocks and the water rushed over him.

Oh, boy, I said to myself. This is going from bad to worse.

I grabbed his dripping sweater just in time, as the wave was dragging him out to sea. I pulled him out of the water, farther up on the shore. I was

worried about another wave. But the sea was calm again, as if it had only one big wave in it, and that wave had gone after my brother, on purpose.

My brother looked as if he were half-drowned. He had seaweed in his hair, and he was shivering.

Then we saw our parents walking slowly towards us, coming out of the fog, holding hands and acting romantic. They had been there the whole time.

My mother ran and put her arms around my brother.

"What happened to you?"

"He was attacked by a wave," I told them, "while we were looking for *you*."

"It must have been a sneaker wave," my father explained. "Come on, we'll get him into some dry clothes."

The next thing I knew, we were in the car with the heater on full-blast, and my brother in the front seat, and we were driving into the little town near Punta Reyes, in search of a Laundromat. The only problem was that my brother didn't have a change of clothes in the car. He had to undress, and my mother wrapped him in the checkered tablecloth we had used for our picnic a couple hours ago, back when the weather was warm. He sat on a plastic chair in the Laundromat and stared at his clothes going around and around in the dryer, as if he was afraid someone would steal them.

"A sneaker wave," my father told him, as if the science of waves would cheer him up, "is a wave that suddenly gets bigger than all the others, and *whoosh!* — it sneaks up on you. It happens because of the tides and the shape of the ocean floor."

My brother sat there in his tablecloth. He didn't care about why there were sneaker waves. He just wanted to get his clothes back on.

My father put his arm around him.

"You know we'd never, ever leave you like that," he promised.

That helped cheer him up a little. My poor brother! He would need a vacation after all this was over.

Six

*Tumbling tumbleweeds nearly crush us
in an Arizona sandstorm*

Our travels had taken us east and west, but now my parents were eager for something new. Something completely crazy, like going to the desert in the hottest part of the summer.

"Something off the beaten track," my father said, spreading out a road map of North America on the living-room rug.

"A place with greater vistas," my mother said, closing her eyes, as if she could see those vistas already, in her imagination.

Did we have a say in their plans, my brother

and I? What if we wanted something on the beaten track? But, as usual, we were prisoners of our parents.

My father pointed at the map. "Let's go to the Southwest," he decided. "Down by the border."

The border with Mexico, that is.

Then he began to sing. "*In a little town, just the other side of the border…*"

That's another thing about my father. He loves to sing. He knows all the words to old songs nobody has ever heard of, the greatest hits from 1965, or something like that, but unfortunately for us, he has a voice like a rusty gate. We keep on telling him that all the time, but he just keeps on singing.

The places he wanted to go looked really small on the map. That meant only one thing. There would be no airports nearby, so we would have to drive there. Already, I imagined the long days in the hot car.

There are all kinds of ways of making the time go faster when you're in a car — besides asking if we're there yet. There are car snacks, for instance. You know, chips or Fritos or chocolate bars or red licorice twists. But in our family, all we get to munch on are carrot and celery sticks, with spring water to wash it down. That sure does fill you up when you're hungry!

Then there's fighting. My little brother and I can always find something to fight about. At first it was Twenty Questions or the Alphabet Game. But our mother wouldn't let us play that any more. He and I figured out we could fight over what CD we would play in my Discman. But when the batteries died, we couldn't even fight over that.

Then there's the radio. My father wants to listen to baseball games, even if he doesn't know the teams or the players. My mother wants classical music. My brother and I want real music, that my father calls "all that crashing and banging."

So we have to compromise. We usually end up with some serious talk show, with people discussing how bad things are in other parts of the world. That sure makes the time go by more quickly!

Then we have to choose a motel. I hoped that, this time, since we were going to be in the desert, we'd get a motel with a swimming pool. A pool and an ice machine, and maybe a playground with monkey bars where my brother could go ape after our day in the car.

But when we finally got off the road, it was so late that all the good motels with swimming pools were filled up. So the only exercise we got that evening was jumping up and down on the beds and having a pillow fight. That is, until my parents couldn't stand it anymore. Then we went to sleep.

On that trip, I learned that if you happen to be in the desert, and the sky turns yellow, you know you're in trouble. You know you're going to have an adventure. Especially in the desert, in the month of August, when the weather is at its hottest.

Since we were in the state of Arizona, my brother and I wanted to see the Grand Canyon. Maybe, just this once, we'd get to go someplace other people went to. I wanted to have a bumper sticker on our car that said, "I visited the Grand Canyon."

But that would have been too easy. I knew what my father was going to say. And sure enough, he said it.

"Anyone can go to the Grand Canyon. It's full of tourists. I read about this other canyon…"

And that's how we decided — or *he* decided — to go to the Canyon de Chelly. Of course. It was different. To begin with, the name was spelled "Chelly," which should rhyme with "jelly." But instead, it was pronounced "shay." Don't ask me why.

"On the way, we can see the Petrified Forest

and the Painted Desert," my father announced. "They're some of the wonders of the world."

Amazing, I thought. Even I had heard of those places before. They were almost as famous as the Grand Canyon. We were actually going to go to a place other people went to.

Of course, it wasn't that simple. It never is with our family.

On our way to the Painted Desert, not too far from a town called Winslow, the sun disappeared. It was the middle of the afternoon, but the sky turned black. Then it turned yellow.

"The sky looks like a bruise," my brother said.

"That can't be a good sign," my mother said, getting worried.

"It says here in the guidebook that the month of August is monsoon season. That's when they have the biggest storms, and the most rain."

"You mean it rains in the desert?" my brother asked. "I thought it was always dry."

"Maybe we'll have a sandstorm, too."

"It's going to rain sand?"

"Don't worry, it's just a little storm," my father said. He sounded very sure of himself. "It'll pass over, you'll see. We're not too far from the Painted Desert."

"I don't like this," my mother said. "Not one little bit."

That's when the car began to shake in the wind, as if it wanted to take off with us inside and fly through the air like in *Twister*. Or maybe *The Wizard of Oz*. I liked that movie better.

Across the desert, a yellow curtain began moving towards us. Behind it, the sun was a smear of light.

"Uh-oh," my father said. "I've never seen that before."

That was the first time I'd ever heard him sound scared. Except, of course, for the time with the alligators in Okefenokee Swamp.

I noticed that we were the only car heading into the storm. All the other cars were going the other way. Then suddenly, so many weird things started to happen at the same time that I couldn't tell which one was weirder.

First, the road completely disappeared in the darkness. Then the sand beat against the car as if it were trying to take all the paint off. No matter how tightly I rolled up the window, the sand got inside the car, and inside my mouth, and it stuck in the back of my throat. If there had been street-lights in the middle of the desert, they would

have gone on, because the sky was darker than night.

Bang! From out of the darkness, I saw something come running at us and hit the car, but I couldn't tell what it was. *Bang!* It came out of nowhere, but this time I saw what it was. The kind of thing you see only in movies.

"My God, what's that?" my mother whispered.

"Giant tumbleweeds," I told her.

"Tumble-whats?" my brother wanted to know.

"They're just a bunch of dried, rolled-up branches, but they're pretty mean."

"I'd like to head off into the sunset, like a tumbling tumbleweed," my father sang in his off-key voice.

He was trying to take our minds off the storm, but meanwhile, he had his face pressed against the inside of the windshield, trying to see through the sandstorm and the dark clouds.

Bang! Another tumbleweed hit us, then bounded away. It was going a lot faster than we were, since it had the wind at its back.

"I don't see any sunset," I told him. "I don't see anything at all."

"Hey, I know that song," my brother shouted over the noise of the wind. "I heard it in a cowboy movie once."

"You three are going to drive me crazy!" my mother yelled. If we had been in a cartoon, she would have torn her hair out.

The sand and rain were coming in sideways, tumbleweeds as big as garbage trucks were hitting our car, the sky had gone purplish-black and the wind was howling like in a horror movie. Not to mention the rivers that were pouring out of the hills and flooding the road.

"The storm can't go on forever," my father said cheerfully. But his knuckles were turning white on the steering wheel.

"Oh, why not?" my brother complained.

Bang! Bang! The car lurched.

"I think those were tumble-twins," my brother said.

Then my mother had had enough.

"I want you to turn around — right now!" she told my father.

And amazingly, that's exactly what he did. He probably wanted to the whole time. We got in line with all the other cars whose drivers had given up on the Painted Desert, and who were heading back to the town of Winslow.

It was quiet in the town when we finally reached it. The storm had passed, but there wasn't a light on anywhere. The power lines were lying like enormous spaghetti on the main street. Which reminded my little brother that he was hungry.

It's not easy finding a restaurant in the middle of a power failure. There was only one place open, but the food was great. We ate tacos and burritos by candlelight.

"How romantic!" my mother said, as she bit into her taco.

There was a double rainbow as big as the desert hanging in the sky. I wondered whether the tumbleweeds were tumbling into the sunset, like in a cowboy picture. The day ended like a movie, with red and yellow and orange rays of light in the west.

All that was missing was a cowboy riding off into the sunset on his horse.

"Look at the colors," my mother exclaimed. "They're so beautiful!"

When she starts talking about how beautiful everything is, it's a sure sign she's feeling better.

Oh, did I mention it? We actually got a motel with a swimming pool that night, just outside the town.

"For being so brave," my father said.

The next day, we finally did see the Painted Desert, on the way to the Canyon de Chelly. The rain had mixed up all the colors, like in a giant paint box.

When my brother and I grow up, we're going to the Grand Canyon. You can count on that!

SEVEN

We are nearly shot full of holes on New Year's Eve in the town of Tehuantepec, Mexico

*M*y mother decided we would have a different kind of Christmas that year. An original kind of Christmas. With no tree, no Santa, no turkey dinner, no stockings and no Boxing Day sale.

What was our present? A trip to Mexico.

We started out by flying to the city of Oaxaca. The name is easy to pronounce. *Wah-hah-cah.* Simple, right?

People do some pretty strange things with food in Oaxaca. They make a black sauce out of chocolate and hot chilies and spread it on chicken. They eat fried grasshoppers, too. Grasshoppers taste a little like potato chips. The only thing I didn't like about them was that the antennae get stuck between your teeth.

My brother didn't like that, either. He would sit in the restaurant, plucking the antennae off each grasshopper, and placing the bodies carefully in rows on his plate. Then he would eat them one by one, with his eyes tightly closed.

Then there were the radishes. In Oaxaca, people grow huge radishes, not to eat, but to make sculptures out of them. There are monsters, churches, musicians, villages, saints — all sculpted out of radishes. Then a few days before Christmas, everyone meets up in the main square to look at the radish sculptures. Of course, the best sculpture wins a prize.

Now that's what I call playing with your food!

Every night there were parades with people on stilts and floats made out of crêpe paper, and fireworks going off everywhere.

And piñatas, too. It was just like the stories we read in Spanish class. The piñata hangs from a pole or the branch of a tree, and a kid who's blindfolded has to hit it with a stick to break it open, so that all the candies and little presents fall out.

It looks simple, but it's not, because the adults keep pushing the piñata just out of reach of the kid who has to hit it. I know — I tried it.

After Christmas in Oaxaca, my parents decided we should go somewhere else for New Year's.

"Hmmm," said my father, squinting at the guidebook. He needs glasses, but he won't admit it. Sometimes we even get lost because he can't read the road map. "It says here that Tehuantepec has one of the most famous markets in Mexico."

"I think I've eaten enough grasshoppers for one trip," said my brother.

"No, no, it says here that the specialty is iguana," my father went on. "Sounds interesting."

"Well, I guess we'd better go there," I said as a joke.

"Great idea! Tehuantepec, here we come!" he yelled.

And he went right out to look for a car to rent. That's the problem with my parents. When you make a joke, they always take it seriously.

So off we went, in search of Tehuantepec.

This time I got to sit up front with my father. My mother sat in the back seat with her eyes half-closed. The day before she'd eaten something that hadn't liked her at

all. That happens sometimes when you travel in Mexico. The food is part of the adventure.

Every time my father hit a bump in the road, and there were more bumps than there was road, she would moan, "*Huevos Motul.*" That was the name of the dish she'd eaten. Some kind of eggs that had come from a chicken in a really bad mood.

By the end of the day, we reached Tehuantepec. And this wasn't just any day, either. It was New Year's Eve. We were going to ring in the New Year in a town where everyone ate iguana. Which, by the way, is some kind of giant lizard. Now that's a really great idea!

As we drove into the center of the town, a gang of kids ran across the street in front of us, dragging a man who was on fire.

"*El viejo año!*" the kids were shouting.

My mother half opened her eyes. "Oh, my God, what are they doing to that poor man?" she whispered.

"Are they killing him?" asked my little brother. "Is he dead?"

Since I'm learning Spanish at school, I knew that *el viejo año* means "the old year." And I also saw that the guy they were dragging down the street was made out of straw and rags.

I was about to tell my mother that, but she'd already closed her eyes again. When you have a bad stomachache, nothing else matters.

We finally found a hotel. It was a pretty strange place. There was no pipe under the sink, so when you washed your hands and face, the water ran onto the floor and splashed your feet. That way, you could wash your hands and feet together. It saved a lot of time, I guess.

"I think I'll have a little rest before dinner," my mother said in a tiny voice.

"Why don't you kids go exploring?" my father suggested.

"But I'm hungry," my brother said.

"Don't worry," I told him. "Maybe we can find you some barbecued iguana, or a cactus sandwich."

"What's an iguana, anyway?"

"A giant lizard that lives in the trees."

"I'm not *that* hungry," my brother said.

We went out the door before my father could tell us to be careful. He always says that. Even if we're just going out to play in the backyard.

There were more strange things about the hotel. Downstairs, in the yard, there was a monkey with a long tail and a sad face. He hopped over to us.

"*No tengo bananas,*" I told him.

"What did you say?"

"That I didn't have any bananas."

"I don't like it when I can't understand," my little brother said. And he pulled his baseball cap down over his eyes. A Houston Astros cap. He didn't know anything about the team, but he liked the star on the cap.

Along with the monkeys, there were turkeys in the yard. They took themselves very seriously, walking around with their chests all puffed up, like they were all the presidents of some country. My brother was afraid of getting bitten.

"Don't worry," I told him. "They're not smart enough to bite you. Did you know that when it rains, turkeys look up with their mouths open to see where the rain is coming from, and they drown?"

"But it's not raining," he said.

He did have a point.

I figured that there would be restaurants in the market, maybe even a fried iguana stand, and that we could find something to eat. Unfortunately, we couldn't find the market.

"Go ahead, ask somebody," he kept pestering me. "You're supposed to know Spanish."

But all of a sudden, I couldn't remember any words. I guess my Spanish was only good for talking to monkeys.

A very small man driving a motorized tricycle passed us in the street. He was pulling a little trailer, and standing in the trailer were two very large women, wrapped in purple shawls, with their hair all swept up, as swirly as the top of a Dairy Queen ice-cream cone. They were wearing little pieces of mirrors in their hair, and they looked like queens.

The next thing we knew, another tricycle buzzed by, pulling four even larger women on a trailer. They had mirrors in their hair, too, and they were wearing all kinds of ornaments, like Christmas trees.

I guess that's how people celebrate New Year's Eve in Tehuantepec.

At the end of the street was the park, and the center of town. There were scraggly palm trees with Christmas lights hanging in them. And people selling just about everything: balloons, flags, ice-cream bars, peanuts, candy and confetti. But no iguanas.

We watched men playing a game with dice and cups. You had to guess which dice were under which cups, or something like that. But before I could figure out how the game worked, someone shouted, "*Policía!*" and everyone ran away.

"Where are they going?" my brother wanted to know.

"I don't know. Home for dinner, maybe?"

"I'm hungry, remember?" my brother reminded me.

Ka-bang! A firecracker exploded really close to us. *Ka-bang!* Another one, right at our feet. Then another, a little farther away this time. My brother forgot all about being hungry.

"We're under attack!" he shouted.

I saw the same gang of kids who had been pulling the straw man through the streets. There wasn't much left of the man, just a few smoking rags at the end of a rope. I guess the old year really was finished.

Now the kids were lighting firecrackers and throwing them at people. I guess that was another New Year's Eve custom in Tehuantepec. I didn't like it very much.

"Let's go back to the hotel," I said to my brother. And this time, he didn't complain.

There was a restaurant next to the hotel. My mother had rice for dinner. Plain rice, with a cup of tea.

I had chicken. So did my brother. There was no iguana on the menu.

"That's okay," my father said. "They say iguana tastes like chicken."

When we finally got back to the hotel, it was very late, and we were very full. The monkey came hopping over to see us. This time I was ready. I had some pieces of banana in a paper napkin. They were fried bananas, but the monkey didn't mind.

"It's nearly midnight," my mother suggested. "Let's go up on the roof. Maybe there'll be fireworks."

She must have been feeling better. Up the stairs we went. The roof was flat, and it was made out of smooth concrete, like the other floors of the building. My father said that the owner had probably planned to build a three-story hotel, but he ran out of money, so he stopped at two for the time being.

Guess what we found on the roof? A goat. A baby goat, to go along with the hungry monkey and the flock of turkeys. The goat wanted to come and see us, but he was behind a wire fence. He had plenty to eat, and a little house to sleep in, but he looked lonely. I guess he didn't have many friends up here. I put my fingers through the fence and he

licked them so hard it tickled. I still had hot sauce on them from dinner. But I guess the goats in Tehuantepec like hot sauce.

Pow! Pow! Bang!

"We're under attack!" my brother shouted again.

"Hit the dirt!" my father ordered.

There wasn't any dirt, so we got down on the concrete. Church bells started ringing. I stuck my head out from behind a pillar. Down below, there were men in the park, shooting their pistols into the air. Firecrackers were nothing compared to this.

"It must be midnight," my father said, as if people shooting their guns at us were the most natural thing in the world. "Happy New Year, kids!"

And he crawled over to my mother on his hands and knees and kissed her.

A couple of bullets passed right overhead. I guess that made the moment more romantic. The goat was smarter than my father. He'd gone and hidden in his house.

"Don't worry," I told my brother. "Tomorrow we'll have iguana flakes for breakfast. It'll be fun, you'll see."

"I can't wait," he grumbled.

CHAPTER EIGHT

We nearly get caught in the latest Mexican revolution

*W*hen it comes to danger, Mexico has got every other place beat. After we survived New Year's Eve in Tehuantepec, my parents wanted to head farther south, towards San Juan Chamula. That's where we got caught up in something even more dangerous.

From Tehuantepec, we had to drive up into the mountains. Even though we were going south, the air was getting colder by the minute. The people we saw were wearing bright wool ponchos, but they were barefoot. I guess if you don't have any shoes, your feet get used to the cold. At least, I hope so.

Clouds were beginning to gather around the tops of the mountains.

"Do you think it's going to snow?" I asked.

My father didn't answer. He was too busy. With one hand on the wheel, he was squinting at the map and grumbling, as if it were the map's fault that he couldn't read it.

"Look," my father said, "this road ends at Chenaló. At least, I think it does. Let's go and have a look."

"What will we do when we get there?" my little brother asked.

"We'll come back," I told him.

"I don't get it," he said.

"You will when you get to be my age."

As usual, I started to read the guidebook. My brother won't, because he doesn't like to try and say all the foreign names. My father was busy driving, and my mother gets a headache if she tries to read in the car.

"Hey, look at this! It says here that the Tzotzil Indians don't like to have their photos taken. They think it's like stealing their souls. Some tourists got killed trying to take pictures."

"Wow!" my brother said. "But how will we remember what we saw?"

"We can remember in our hearts," my mother told him.

"Do photographs really steal your soul?" he asked.

"They do if you think they do," my mother told him.

My brother was very quiet. A little while later, he said, "I think I'll skip my next class picture."

It was too bad we couldn't take any pictures, because the countryside really was pretty. There were tall green hills covered in forests, with fields built on platforms up and down the slopes. The platforms were called terraces, and they had been built centuries ago.

"Look at those trees," I said to my brother. "Real bananas are growing in them."

"I thought bananas came from the store," he said. I think he was just joking, though you never know.

The road climbed up one side of a hill, and was about to coast down the other when my mother said, "Look at that view! It's so beautiful."

"We'll stop here," my father said.

He pulled off the road. We all got out of the car. My father put rocks in front of the tires, just in case the brake didn't work. The green hills seemed to go on forever, with higher mountains in the distance, and clouds stuck on top of them.

"Those clouds look like big fluffy hats," my mother said.

"There's no one around," my father decided. "Nobody's soul to steal. We can take a picture."

"Don't," my mother told him. "Remember, these people take that seriously."

My father took out his camera from his pocket anyway. He aimed it at the hills and terraces below.

Suddenly, my brother shouted, "Look, down there!"

On the terrace just beneath us, where the banana trees grew, people were lying on the ground, face down, with their ponchos over their heads. They really didn't want their souls stolen, not one little bit.

"Did you take a picture?" my mother asked.

"No," my father said. "I didn't have time to."

"We're leaving. Now."

We all got into the car. But when we tried to drive away, the car wouldn't move.

"Something's wrong," my father said, worried.

"Maybe the Tzotzil people cast a magic spell on us," my brother suggested.

"I think I know what it is."

I squeezed out of the back seat. You can't be any fatter than a string of spaghetti to get in and out of a two-door rented car.

Then I went around to the front of the car and kicked the two big stones away from the tires. My mother started laughing as I got back inside. So did my brother. My father concentrated on his driving.

As we drove past the first terrace, I saw that all the people had gotten up again, and were working in their fields. That was a close call!

At the bottom of the valley was a crossroads. One of the directions led to Chenaló. But it didn't look as though we were going to get there. Big rocks were blocking the road, and on those rocks were men wearing scarves over their faces. When we got closer, I could see that they weren't much older than I was. And they all had guns.

"Chenaló?" my father asked.

"*Ustedes no pasan*," they said. "Not for you."

"Why not? *Por qué?*"

They stared at us. I guess *Why?* was not a question they were used to answering. They pointed in the other direction.

"Chamula," they said.

"Were they soldiers?" my little brother asked as my father turned the car around. "They didn't have uniforms."

"I don't think so," my mother told him. "I think they were ordinary people, trying to get their land back."

"Back from who?" my brother asked.

"The people who work on the land don't own it. And they don't always get a fair price for what they grow, like those bananas you saw. In a lot of villages, they don't even have schools or clean water. I think the guys blocking the road are trying to change that."

My brother was quiet for a minute or two. And let me tell you, that doesn't happen very often.

And that was how we ended up visiting San Juan Chamula, another town that's famous for being a place where you can't take pictures. There were signs in several languages, warning people to keep their cameras in their pockets.

There did not seem to be very much to see in Chamula. We went into the church to look at the paintings. It was very dark inside, but when my eyes got used to the darkness, I could see that this church was different from other churches we had visited. Very different. First of all, the benches had been taken out, and the floor was covered with fir-tree branches. The statues of the saints, that usually sit on pedestals, were standing right on the floor, along with the paintings that are usually on the walls.

People were praying to the saints so hard they didn't even notice us. They had burning candles stuck in Coke bottles in front of the statues, next to squares of chocolate and little piles of chili peppers. It wasn't like any church I'd ever seen.

We didn't spend more than a minute in there.

It felt as though we had wandered into someone else's house, where we didn't belong.

"Did those guys who were blocking the road change around the church, too?" my brother wondered.

"Maybe," my mother said. "It looks like the Indian people are taking back the church and using it in their own way, just the way they want to take back the land."

"It looks like they put a different religion inside that church," I said.

"It was spooky," my brother decided. "Nobody even looked at us."

We sat down on a fountain in front of the church to figure out what to do next. We still felt the spookiness from the church, even my parents. The fountain was dry, as if there hadn't been any water in it for ages.

In no time at all, we were surrounded by a dozen little girls from the village. They were pointing at my brother and laughing.

"*Rubio! Rubio!*" they cried.

"What are they saying?" my brother wanted to know.

"Something about rubies?" my mother wondered.

I pulled out my pocket dictionary. Along with the guidebook, it was really very useful.

"*Rubio...* That means blond. I guess they don't see blond kids very often."

My brother took his Astros cap out of his backpack and put it on. He pulled it down as far as he could.

"I don't like this place," he said. "Not at all. Everything's too strange here."

All of a sudden a soccer ball came sailing in our direction. I jumped up and knocked it down with my chest so that it fell at my feet, the way my coach at home taught us to do. The ball was old and held together with tape. I looked up and saw a group of boys standing and watching me. I kicked the ball back to them.

"*Gracias,*" they said.

You can meet people anywhere in the world if you know how to play soccer.

Then one of the little girls who was braver than the rest of them ran up to my mother, reached up and touched her hair. My mother smiled and shook her blond curly hair. The little girl dashed back to her friends. All of them were giggling. Our hair sure made a big impression on them.

Two women came out of the church. One was wearing a long purple scarf on her head, and the other had a brightly colored bag over her shoulder. They were no taller than my little brother. The women clapped their hands and shouted something at the girls, and they laughed one last time before scattering off in all directions.

I never expected the women would walk right up to us. They certainly weren't shy, not like the girls. One of them reached into her bag and took out four cloth bracelets. She put a bracelet around each of our wrists.

We were too surprised to move, except for my mother, who held out her arm. Suddenly Chamula didn't seem so strange and scary anymore.

"Friendship bracelets," she said. "Aren't they beautiful?"

My father reached into his pocket to give them some money, but the women shook their heads.

Just then, I saw something flying toward us out of the corner of my eye. It was the soccer ball again. I leaped up and headed it straight into the air. When it came down, I gave it a bicycle kick back to the group of boys.

They applauded — it was a pretty fancy move. Maybe my brother didn't like Chamula, but it was all right with me.

When the day was over, we left the town and drove out of the mountains, back down to where the air was warmer. That night we stayed in a big hotel that even had a television set. My father said we'd earned it.

The news came on the TV. We couldn't understand what the announcer was saying, and I didn't have time to look up all the words in my pocket dictionary. The announcer sounded very serious, as if something very important had happened. Pictures of men with guns standing by the side of a road came on the screen. They were wearing scarves over their faces.

"Hey, I know those guys!" my brother said.

Then we saw the church at Chamula. A man with a scarf over his face was standing on the edge of the fountain where we had sat, holding a very mean-looking rifle, and giving a speech.

"It's the revolution," my father said. "Imagine that, we just missed it."

We'll remember Chamula for sure — with or without pictures!

NINE

Slaughter Canyon Cave nearly lives up to its name

*O*ne of the strangest trips we ever took started off with a close encounter. I think it was of the Third Kind, just like in the movie. Now, I don't know if you believe in extraterrestrials. You know, those little green men from outer space.

Okay, maybe they're not green, but they do come from outer space. And according to what I read in the guidebook, the only time they actually landed on earth was just outside Roswell, New Mexico. It's the little green men capital of the world.

We weren't actually looking for extraterrestrials. We had returned to the Southwest desert country when we happened to drive through Roswell, on our way to the Carlsbad Caverns.

First we saw the sign for the town. Then all of a sudden, we were surrounded by little green men. They were on posters, billboards and cardboard cut-outs. Inflatable plastic big green men were floating in the air above us. I saw an Outer Space Café and an Aliens Only Laundromat.

Extraterrestrials sure had a good nose for business. The whole town of Roswell was covered in green signs.

"I think we should stop for ice cream," my father suggested.

My brother looked out the window suspiciously.

"I'm not very hungry," he said.

"Since when do you have to be hungry to eat ice cream?" my father asked.

"Don't worry," I told my brother. "There won't be any aliens. Look, are any of those people green?"

"What if they're disguised? How can we tell?"

"Their antennae. They'd be sticking out from underneath their baseball caps."

"Very funny," my brother said.

We went into the ice-cream shop. My brother stared very hard at the man who served us our ice cream. It was bright green, of course. E. T. flavor.

"Does this ice cream come from outer space?" my brother asked, staring at the man's cap.

"Of course," said my mother. "It came by flying saucer. What does it taste like?"

"It's out of this world," I answered.

My little brother laughed so hard he snorted green ice cream up his nose.

Then he wanted to send a postcard to Miro. A postcard with a picture of a little green man, of course.

"Miro's never seen one," he said. "He'll think it's so cool."

Even after my visit to Roswell, I still haven't made up my mind about people from outer space. Part of me wants to believe in them, and part of me doesn't. But you have to admit, it would be really interesting to meet one.

The Carlsbad Caverns are one of the wonders of the world, an enormous chain of caves deep under the ground. That sounded pretty good to my brother and me.

Everything was going well until my father picked up the guidebook while he was eating his ice cream, put his glasses on his nose and started reading.

"Hmm," he said. "Three million people visit the caves every summer. The inside is entirely lit up. There are guardrails everywhere and a little train that takes you from room to room. There's a welcome center, a souvenir shop and a snack-bar."

My brother and I looked at each other. Now that sounded great!

My father closed the book. "I'm sure we can do better than that."

"Oh, no," we groaned.

That's how we ended up visiting Slaughter Canyon Cave. "No facilities," I read in the guidebook once we climbed back into the car and started driving across the desert and around the mountains. Giant cactuses grew along the road, poking their heads out of fields of black volcanic lava.

"What's that mean?" my little brother asked.

"It means no snackbars, no souvenir stands, no roads and no water. And no toilets."

"What if I have to —."

"You go behind a rock. Just watch out for rattle — !"

Ka-boom!

The car started shaking and bouncing, as if we were driving down a railroad track.

"Nobody panic!" my father ordered in a loud voice.

My mother grabbed on to the door handle and closed her eyes.

He wrestled with the steering wheel to keep the car on the road, and finally we came to a stop. We all got out and looked. One of the back tires was shredded. Pieces of rubber lay all over the pavement.

"A flat tire!" my father groaned.

"I guess there aren't any gas stations around here," my mother said, shading her eyes and looking out across the totally empty, totally hot desert.

"We'll just change it ourselves," my father declared.

There was only one problem. My father had never changed a tire. In Mexico, our car engine blew up and a drunk man tried to fix it with a spoon. In Georgia, a flying rock shattered our back window. But we had never had a flat tire before. In all our travels, that was the only thing that hadn't happened to us.

"There's a first time for everything," my father said cheerfully. "Anyone can do it."

Well, almost anyone. My father took the jack and the spare tire and a tool with four arms out of the trunk and laid them on the ground. Then he rubbed his chin and looked up and down the road, as if help might come driving up.

But there was no help. There was nobody else on the road. All the other cars were on the other road, the one that went to the Carlsbad Caverns.

"There has to be a way of doing this," he said. "A very logical way."

But my father isn't the most logical person in the world. When he had to figure out how to do something, like putting together a piece of furniture that came unassembled, he started thinking so quickly and so hard that the furniture never looked like it did in the picture on the box.

That's when I had an idea. A logical idea.

In the glove compartment, there was a little book that told you everything you needed to know about the car. The Owner's Manual, it was called. I'm a logical kind of person, so I looked in the table of contents.

"If You Have a Flat Tire," it said.

"Step one," I read out loud. "Park on a level spot."

No problem there. The desert was absolutely flat.

"Firmly set the parking brake."

My mother reached into the car and did that.

"Remove the wheel ornament."

We stood around looking for a while before we realized that the Owner's Manual was talking about the hubcap.

"It says here to avoid unexpected personal injury," I added.

"Now that's a good idea," my mother said.

"Insert the jack at the correct jack points," I told him. "And don't climb under the car."

"Who's Jack?" my brother asked. But nobody was in the mood to laugh.

It's amazing the useful things you can learn from a little book like this one. Luckily, the instructions were written for people who had never changed a tire before.

Step by step, we changed the tire. I read the instructions, and my father followed them. More or less. Every time I told him what to do next, he asked me, "Are you sure?" And every time, my mother gave him one of her looks, and said, "Honey, he knows how to read."

Still, it took a long time. Wavy lines of heat rose up from the desert, and they made my head spin. It was enough to make you see little green men. I couldn't believe that the tiny, shaky-looking contraption called a jack could lift a big heavy car like ours. But it did.

"Remember to replace the tools in the trunk when finished," I read from the book.

"Obviously," my father said.

Two very hot hours later, four very red-faced people continued on their way.

"See?" my father said. "That was easy."

My brother and I groaned and prayed that the

other three tires would hold up. And they did.

A little later, we were bouncing over the rough, rocky roads, on our way to Slaughter Canyon Cave. The cave that hardly anyone ever visits.

"The place doesn't have the friendliest name," my mother pointed out.

"It's named after a Mr. Slaughter. It also says in the guidebook that you have to bring your own flashlight. One flashlight per person. Otherwise they won't let you in."

"We'll find a flashlight somewhere," my father said.

I looked out the window. Rocks and cactus. Cactus and rocks. But no flashlight stores. We should have bought one in Roswell. A green flashlight, of course.

Suddenly the road ended. You know the expression "the middle of nowhere?" That's exactly where we were. There was a parking lot made of rocks and a sign that said Slaughter Canyon Cave, and a couple of rusty pick-up trucks. Nothing else. I guess that's what they mean by No Facilities.

I saw a smaller sign nailed onto a post. There was a list of all the things that could happen to you. Rattlesnake bites. Flash floods. Heat stroke. Lightning storms. Dehydration, which is a fancy word for dying of thirst. No one was allowed beyond this point without a one-quart bottle of water.

We had a bottle, all right. One quart for the four of us. We started walking up the trail.

A minute later, my little brother started saying how thirsty he was. After telling him he had to wait, my father gave in. Of course, my brother drank half the bottle of water. I could just imagine us, dying of thirst in the desert — all of us but him.

The trail kept climbing, which was very strange, since a canyon is supposed to be a low place, and we were going up the side of a mountain. The trail got narrower and narrower as we crept along the side of a cliff. Pretty soon we would have to turn into mountain goats if we wanted to use this trail.

Oh, I forgot to mention something else. My mother is scared of heights.

"Just don't look down," my father told her.

She didn't answer. She was too scared. Meanwhile, to make her even more afraid, my little brother danced along the trail ahead of us, as if he didn't even know there was a cliff at his feet.

Out of nowhere, a woman in a khaki uniform appeared. A park ranger. She looked at us as if we were little green men.

"Coming to visit the cave?" she asked.

"Yes, ma'am," my mother answered. I wondered what else we would be doing here, stuck to the side of the cliff like flies.

"This is the entrance." All I could see was a crack in the mountain. "Where are your flashlights?"

"We don't have one. We thought that —"

"No entry without a flashlight." She looked at us again. "*Four flashlights.*"

"But we came all this way —"

"I'll see what I can do."

Then she disappeared into the crack in the mountain.

"At least she didn't notice that we don't have four bottles of water," my mother whispered.

"I'm thirsty," my brother complained.

Before we could start fighting, the ranger appeared again.

"You're in luck," she said. She handed me a flashlight. "I've only got three. You two will have to share. Which means you'll have to stick together." The ranger gave us a look, and smiled. "Whether you want to or not."

"I'm holding the flashlight," I told my brother.

"No fair!" he complained, and kicked a stone over the edge of the cliff, which you're never supposed to do, because you can't tell who might be walking down below.

We stepped into the cave. It was freezing inside. After the heat of the desert, it was amazing. You could actually see your breath. And it was completely, one hundred percent pitch dark.

With our flashlights showing the way, we started climbing down a long passage. A few other people were with us, the ones who owned the pick-up trucks back in the parking lot, I guess. The park ranger told us that we weren't allowed to eat or drink in the cave. That was okay — we were out of water anyway. We weren't allowed to touch the walls of the cave, either. One smudge of oil from a human hand could stop the stalagmites and stalactites from growing.

Down and down we went. One day, the ranger told us, a man named Mr. Slaughter was taking care of his sheep, and one of them disappeared right into the mountain. He went looking for it, and discovered the entrance to the cave. The mountain we had just climbed was hollow, and we were climbing back down to where we had started.

Along the way, there were all kinds of rock formations. Some of them looked like kings on their thrones. Others looked like Christmas trees. There were rainbow-colored bridges of rock that crossed underground rivers and lakes.

It was so fabulous that even my mother forgot to say how beautiful it was.

"Do you know the difference between stalactites and stalagmites?" the ranger asked me.

"Sure," I told her. "Stalagmites grow from the floor to the ceiling. Stalactites grow the other way around."

"Very good!"

"Everybody knows that!" my brother hissed. He was still mad because I got to hold the flashlight.

Finally, we reached the bottom of the cave. The ranger told us to sit down, shut off our lights and not say a word. We all sat in complete darkness, in total silence, for a minute or two.

I wondered if being blind was like this. I could hear my blood running through my veins, and my heart beating. I thought about the tons of rock hanging over our heads.

Then, from somewhere deep in the cave, a drop of water fell into a pool.

"The sound of eternity," the park ranger said. Then she switched on her light.

We admired the rock formations a little more, making sure not to touch them. Before we began our climb back through the hollow mountain, the ranger counted us. Once, then twice.

Someone was missing. Guess who? It was my little brother.

My mother panicked right away. "Oh, my God, he's lost!"

"Stay calm, honey," my father said. "He can't be far."

The park ranger swept the walls of the cave with her high-powered light. We saw kings on thrones and stone Christmas trees flash by, but not my little brother.

A few seconds later, we heard a voice.

"I am the spirit of Slaughter Canyon. I got slaughtered. *Wooo...!*"

Everybody started laughing, even the park ranger. My brother showed up, smiling a big smile. My mother grabbed his hand. And then we climbed back up toward the little pinhole of light, opening out onto the sky.

By the time we left Slaughter Canyon, it was late in the afternoon. The car was waiting for us, as hot as an oven inside.

"We have a surprise for you," my mother said as we bounced back down the road.

"What is it?" my brother and I asked.

"If I tell you, it won't be a surprise."

I couldn't believe it when we pulled into the parking lot of the Carlsbad Caverns.

We reached the mouth of the main cave just as the sun was going down. A few minutes later, I heard a whispering noise. The whispers were growing louder.

Then, suddenly, millions and millions of bats were pouring out of the cave, flying into the dark sky, on their way to their night's work of eating insects. It was fabulous!

And we'd gotten there just in time.

THE END —

For now

It's February. Outside, the snow is halfway up to the roof. It's even too cold to go skating. Exactly the kind of weather that makes my parents want to plan our next vacation.

And sure enough, what should come in the mail but a postcard. A postcard of red-roofed houses on a rocky island floating in a deep blue sea. A postcard from one of our parents' friends.

My father took out his new glasses, blew the dust off them and started reading it.

"It's from Fred. He's on the island of Krk," he said. Then he turned the card over and looked at the picture. "Hmm, not bad. I've always wanted to go to a place that doesn't have any vowels."

He and my mother got out their travel book. It's a sort of guide that tells you about all the strange and dangerous destinations you can go to if you happen to like out-of-the-way places. My father leafed through it until he found the island of Krk. It was in Croatia, a country I'd never heard of.

I grabbed the book from him.

"Let me see. Hmmm… Beware of dangerous winding roads, with steep precipices on both sides, wild mountain goats and poisonous snakes."

"Sounds fascinating," my mother said, gazing at the postcard.

"It certainly does," my father said, getting excited.

"And the national dish is *blitva*," I continued.

"What's *blitva*?" asked my brother. "Some kind of insect?"

"Sounds like a weed," I told him, "that the mountain goats eat when there's nothing tastier around."

"Yuck," my brother said.

"On the other hand," I told him, "it could be roasted lizard. Or fried cat ears."

My brother hugged Miro.

"Shh! He'll hear you."

"So what do you think?" my parents asked us.

My brother and I looked at one another. An island called Krk. Why not Zut or Iz while you're at it?

We sighed. We couldn't wait.

Krk, here we come!

THE END

Marie-Louise Gay is an author and illustrator of children's books. Her Stella and Sam books have been translated into more than fifteen languages. She has won many major awards, including two Governor General's awards, the Marilyn Baillie Picture Book Award and the Vicky Metcalf Award. She has been nominated twice for the Hans Christian Andersen Award.

Born and raised in Chicago, *David Homel* is an award-winning novelist, screenwriter, journalist and translator. He is a two-time winner of the Governor General's Award for translation and the author of six novels, including *The Speaking Cure* (winner of the Hugh MacLennan Prize and the Jewish Public Library Award for fiction) and, most recently, *Midway*.

Marie-Louise and David live in Montreal, but travel as much as possible.